Teddy
at the Seashore

AMANDA DAVIDSON

Holt, Rinehart and Winston/New York

For Andrew Field

Originally published in Great Britain under the title *Teddy at the Seaside*.

Library of Congress Cataloging in Publication Data
Davidson, Amanda.
Teddy at the seashore.

Summary: A lonely teddy bear gets a surprise visit to the beach.
[1. Teddy bears—Fiction.   2. Beaches—Fiction.
3. Toys—Fiction]   I. Title.
PZ7.D2824Te   1984   [E]   83-22745

ISBN:0-03-071026-X

First American Edition
Printed in Italy
1 3 5 7 9 10 8 6 4 2

ISBN 0-03-071026-X

This is 7 Walnut Grove. Teddy lives here.

Is he downstairs?

No, he is upstairs . . .

in the toy cupboard.

He is lonely.

He has no one to play with.

All of a sudden, Teddy's lifted out . . .

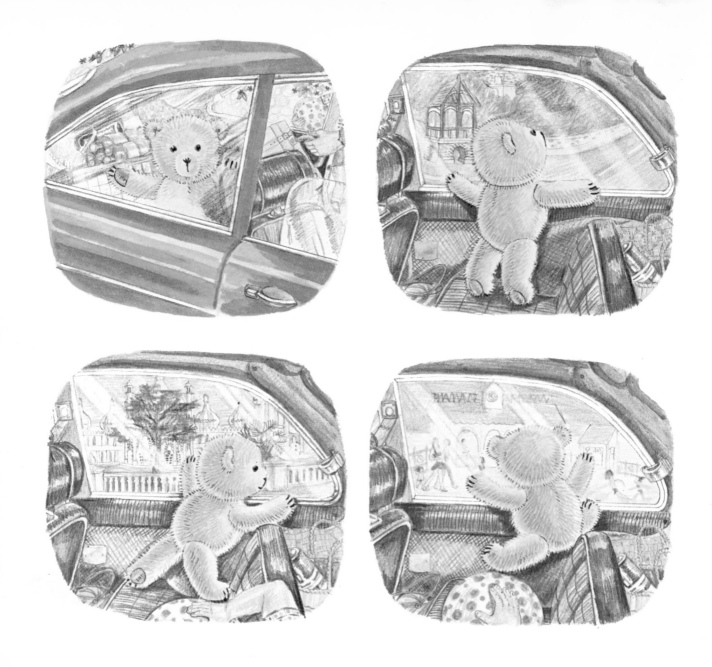

and put in the car.

"Where are we going?" wonders Teddy.

Look, Teddy, there's the sea!

"This is fun!" thinks Teddy.

"What happens next?"

Teddy has a paddle

and a ride in a boat.

Splash! Teddy has fallen into the water.

Never mind, Teddy. You'll soon be dry.

"Hello, seagull," says Teddy.

"Hey, come back. That's our picnic."

"Now look what you've done!"

Cheer up, Teddy. It's time to go home.

A very tired Teddy is ready for bed.